Scc

written by Pam Holden
illustrated by Jim Storey

Grandpa was unhappy and worried because his garden was being visited by hungry birds. Every day they flew over his strawberry patch and watched as the berries slowly began to change from green to pink. As soon as they saw any strawberries turning pink, they quickly flew down to peck holes in them.

Grandpa asked the children to help him keep the birds away, so that the strawberries had a chance to turn red and become ripe and sweet.
"Put your thinking caps on," he told them. "Who can think of a good way to get rid of these birds?"

James and Molly thought hard all day until they had an excellent idea.
"Let's make a scarecrow," they suggested. "Its name means that it scares crows, so it will scare these birds, too."
Grandpa was pleased with their idea. "We will get busy right away," he said. "What will we use to make this scarecrow?"

Grandma gave them a paper bag to make the head.
"Can we have a pair of Grandpa's old trousers and that torn shirt, please?" the children asked. "We'll use newspaper to stuff the body."
James put a stick through the shirt to look like arms.
Then he put a two longer sticks through the body and stuck them into the ground.
Molly found an old hat and a pair of yellow gloves.

When the scarecrow was standing in the garden, the family watched from a window to see what happened. After a while, one bird came flying down near the scarecrow. Then four more birds flew down and began to peck at the strawberries, while one even sat on the scarecrow's head!

The children knew they had to think of another idea.
"We must make our scarecrow scarier!" they decided.
"He stands too still to frighten the birds."
James suggested, "We could add long hair that will blow in the wind."
Grandma found some knitting wool that looked like real hair. Before long, the scarecrow had wild hair blowing around his shoulders.

At first the birds didn't come near it, but they quickly got used to the blowing hair. Nothing bad happened to them when they came back to peck at the strawberries.

"Our scarecrow is too quiet to frighten the birds," said Molly. "Let's add some noise. We could ask Grandma for some tin cans that will rattle in the wind." Grandpa made holes in the tin cans and helped the children tie them onto strings. Soon the scarecrow looked like a tin man with cans hanging from his arms.

For a short time, the birds kept away because of the rattling noise from the swinging tins. But before long they got used to it and came flying back.

Just when the strawberries were nearly ripe, the children thought of another idea to chase the birds away. Grandpa helped them blow up bright balloons of all shapes and sizes. They drew faces on the balloons and gathered them into bunches that they tied to the scarecrow's arms.

The hungry birds watched the scarecrow carefully from their tree, but they didn't wait long before they came swooping down to finish their meal. Suddenly one of the balloons popped with a loud bang. The birds flew up into the sky squawking with fright. Every time a bird came back to the strawberry patch, another balloon popped and sent it flapping away.

Pop!
Pop!
Pop!

By the time the last balloon popped, the strawberries were perfectly ripe. Grandpa and Grandma and the children had a delicious feast.

"Thank you, Scarecrow," they said, "Now you can guard the blueberries for us."